The Valentine Box

The Valentine Box

MAUD HART LOVELACE

ILLUSTRATED BY INGRID FETZ

Thomas Y. Crowell Company

New York

Copyright © 1966 by Maud Hart Lovelace
Illustrations copyright © 1966 by Ingrid Fetz
All rights reserved. No part of this book may
be reproduced in any form, except by a reviewer,
without the permission of the publisher.
Designed by Joan Maestro
Manufactured in the United States of America
Published in Canada by Fitzhenry & Whiteside Limited, Toronto
Library of Congress Catalog No. 66-14942

ISBN 0-690-85659-8
0-690-85660-1 (LB)

6 7 8 9 10

Another version of this story was first published
in Jack and Jill (Curtis Publishing Company).

By the Author

BETSY-TACY • BETSY-TACY AND TIB

BETSY AND TACY GO OVER THE BIG HILL

BETSY AND TACY GO DOWNTOWN • HEAVEN TO BETSY

BETSY IN SPITE OF HERSELF • BETSY WAS A JUNIOR

BETSY AND JOE • CARNEY'S HOUSE PARTY

EMILY OF DEEP VALLEY • THE TUNE IS IN THE TREE

THE TREES KNEEL AT CHRISTMAS

BETSY AND THE GREAT WORLD • BETSY'S WEDDING

THE GOLDEN WEDGE *(with Delos W. Lovelace)*

WHAT CABRILLO FOUND • THE VALENTINE BOX

The Valentine Box

As Janice walked home to lunch on Valentine's Day, she felt <u>unhappy</u>. It was snowing hard, and it occurred to her that perhaps she wouldn't be allowed to go back to school in the afternoon.

That cheered her up, but only for a moment. She remembered that her mother would let her go, if it was possible at all, because of the Valentine Box.

"And that's the very reason I don't want to go, because of the Valentine Box," Janice thought.

It was very mixed up. What made it harder was that she didn't want her mother to know how she was feeling.

The Valentine Box was very beautiful. The fifth graders had made it themselves, covering a pasteboard box with red tissue paper, decorating it with white hearts, and cutting a slit in the top through which they would mail valentines to one another this afternoon. It sat on the teacher's desk, looking gay and important, and most of the children could

hardly wait for the party. But Janice didn't have a single "party" feeling. In fact, she had a lump in her throat.

The trouble was that she was afraid she wouldn't get any valentines. She was new in the town of Oak Grove. She was going to a new school, and she didn't have any friends.

Back in the city where she used to live, she had had plenty of friends, and one very special friend named Mary Lou. Mary Lou had lived in the same apartment house, and they had walked to school together, and after school they had gone roller-skating, or had played games, or with paper dolls.

Mary Lou was still her friend, of course, and they talked with each other on the telephone sometimes, for Oak Grove was a suburb of the city. It was very different,

though. Oak Grove had lawns and trees and shrubs around the pretty new houses, and there was a clean shining new school.

There was a girl in her grade whom Janice would have liked for a friend. Margaret was her name. Margaret was a large, rosy, smiling girl with a mop of curly light-brown hair. She looked full of fun, and her house was just in the next block.

But Margaret had hardly noticed Janice, who was small for her age and quiet. After she got acquainted with people, Janice wasn't quiet. She was as full of fun as anybody. But she didn't get acquainted easily.

"Would you like to go out and find some children to play with?" her mother had suggested a little anxiously once or twice.

But Janice was too shy to do that.

"I don't believe I'll have a single valentine in that box," she thought worriedly now as she hurried home through the thickening snow.

In the doorway she took off her high boots and carried them into the house. A great gust of snow blew in with her.

"Mercy, what a day!" her mother said, brushing the flakes from Janice's new red snowsuit. "I'm thankful for this snowsuit and your boots. If it weren't Valentine's Day, I wouldn't let you go back to school this afternoon. And speaking of valentines, see what came in the morning mail!"

She held up a big square envelope addressed to Janice.

"It's from Mary Lou!" Janice cried joyfully, and after examining the envelope from all sides, she opened it with care. The valentine was beautiful, trimmed with lace paper, and inside it Mary Lou had written, "You are my Valentine, Your friend, Mary Lou." Janice liked that even better than the lace paper. She read it over two or three times.

"This makes three valentines I've gotten," she said to her mother. For there had been valentines from her father and mother on the breakfast table.

"And you may get more in the Valentine Box," her mother answered. She added seriously, "I wouldn't expect many, though, if I were you, Janice. You must remember that you're new in this school."

"Of course," said Janice. "And we're going to have refreshments. That's the important thing."

It wasn't, really. The important thing was getting valentines from friends who really liked you, like Mary Lou.

After Janice had eaten her lunch, she climbed into the red snowsuit again.

"It's snowing so hard," her mother said,

"that I'm going to lend you this old purse to carry your valentines in."

She meant the valentines Janice was taking to school to put in the box for the other children. Janice and her mother had made them together. They had had fun cutting and pasting and coloring, almost as much fun as Janice and Mary Lou had had making them the year before. Janice was giving one to her teacher, and one to Margaret, and one to a little boy called Bobby who had loaned her his eraser. Bobby was friendly with everyone. There were others for children whom she scarcely knew.

"I think I'll take Mary Lou's valentine to school with me," she said suddenly.

"That's a good idea," answered her mother. "You can show it to your teacher."

So Janice put the beautiful lace-paper valentine into her purse with the others. She kissed her mother good-bye and started back to school feeling a little happier. But the happy feeling didn't last. In just a moment the lump was back in her throat.

The weather was even wilder than it had
been before. The wind was blowing the snow
in dizzy circles, whipping the shrubs to and
fro, and tossing the branches of the trees.

Across the street some children were going to school together. They were pushing
one another into the drifts and shouting:
"Giving me a valentine?" "Like fun I am!"
"Bet you are!" "Bet I'm not!"

That was the way Janice and Mary Lou used to joke on the way to school on Valentine's Day.

Janice walked primly along on her side of the street with her mother's purse under her arm. No matter how hard she swallowed, she couldn't swallow that lump. The snow was beating into her face, and once when she wiped it away, she wiped two big tears along with it.

But there wasn't really much chance to cry. She was too busy keeping her feet on the ground and the purse tucked under her arm. The wind was growing stronger all the time, and just as she reached the corner opposite the school, one terrific gust almost sent her into a snowdrift.

"Oh! Oh! Oh!" she heard someone cry.

Whirling around, she saw Margaret in a blue snowsuit with what seemed at first to be a flock of red birds swirling around her head. They were red valentines which the wind had snatched from her hand.

"My valentines!" wailed Margaret. "I've lost them!"

"We can catch them!" Janice shouted.

"We never can!"

"Yes, we can! They're easy to find because they're red."

Ploughing into a drifted lawn Janice rescued one, two, three. Margaret rescued a fourth, and Janice a fifth. It was like a game, and they began to whoop.

The wind entered into the fun. It blew one valentine into a pine tree far over their heads.

"I'll get it!" shrieked Janice.

"Don't you climb that tree! Pines scratch!"

"I'll fly up! I'm Mary Poppins!" And Janice dashed in among the needles, scrambled up the tree and down.

Margaret chased another envelope down someone's cellar window.

"I'm Mary Poppins' sister!" she yelled.
They had a glorious time.
"There's one more," cried Margaret.
The wind had veered, and the last red en-
velope was blowing up the street. It skipped

like a naughty child turning its back on school. Margaret and Janice tumbled after the truant.

They couldn't run fast because of the snow, and the wind kept the envelope always ahead of them. Sometimes it would rest for a tantalizing moment on a drift, but just as they caught up, it would flutter away.

Back at the school, a bell rang.

"Janice!" cried Margaret. "Go back to school! You'll be late."

"No later than you'll be," Janice called. "I'm going to catch that valentine if it's the last thing I do."

The valentine blew on, tempting them to follow, leading them farther and farther from the school.

On the lawn before one of the houses someone had been building a snowman. He was a wonderful, fat snowman with a pipe stuck into his mouth. Now the wind veered again and blew the red envelope smack against his head. It stuck there, low on one side, like a jaunty cap. Janice and Margaret screamed with laughter.

Then Margaret grabbed the envelope and took Janice's hand, and they raced for the schoolhouse.

The hall was warm and unnaturally quiet. The doors on either side were closed. Margaret and Janice brushed the snow from each other, giggling.

"Your feet are sopping," Janice whispered.

"But we got all my valentines, I think. Let's count."

Taking off her wet mittens, Margaret laid the damp red envelopes in a row on the hall radiator. Together she and Janice counted them off. One for Miss Merrill, one for Bobby, others for John, Carol, Beverly, Peter . . .

There wasn't one for Janice. Janice and

Margaret noticed that at the same moment.

"It's too bad they're wet," Janice said hastily. "Mom gave me a purse to carry mine in . . ." She broke off with a gasp. "Where *is* it?"

"What?"

"My purse. I must have dropped it while I was chasing the valentines."

They stared at each other in dismay.

"Don't you worry!" Margaret said. "We'll go right back and find it."

"No," said Janice. "We'd better go and tell Miss Merrill first. We're late enough already."

Miss Merrill was sympathetic, especially after Margaret explained exactly what happened.

"Did you have anything of value in the purse, Janice?" she asked.

"My valentines for the Valentine Box," said Janice. "And one other. It came from Mary Lou, my best friend back in the city."

Miss Merrill looked thoughtful. She put her hands on the shoulders of the new red snowsuit and looked down at the stout rubber boots.

"You're perfectly snug," she said. "And there's time enough for you to run back and take a look."

"May I go along to help hunt?" Margaret asked. "It's on account of me she lost it, you know."

Miss Merrill looked at Margaret's rubbers, which were oozing snow.

"No," she said. "Because your feet are wet. But Bobby may go to help Janice if he wants to."

"Sure," said Bobby. "I'll go."

He put on his boots and his warm jacket and cap, and he and Janice went out into the snow. Janice felt shy at first but as they went up the street, she told him about the fun she and Margaret had had, and they both started laughing. They reached the snowman who had worn the red valentine cap.

"Oh, boy!" said Bobby when she told him about that. "I wish I'd seen him." He stopped and pointed. "Lookee!"

There at the snowman's feet lay Janice's mother's purse. Janice ran to pick it up, and it wasn't hurt at all. The valentines inside were perfectly dry. She took one out.

"This is from my friend Mary Lou in the city," she said, showing it to him.

"Gee, that's neat!" Bobby replied. "Did you like living in the city?"

"Yes, I did," Janice answered.

"Well," said Bobby. "You can't beat Oak Grove. You're going to like Oak Grove, too, after you live here a while."

Janice began to think that she would after they were back in the schoolroom and had taken off their wraps and she had put her valentines into the box. For Miss Merrill asked her to be postman.

Janice almost choked with excitement and

pleasure as she went up to the front of the room and lifted the cover from the big gay Valentine Box.

She took out the letters one by one and called out the names:

"Margaret. Peter. Carol. Bobby. Beverly. Miss Merrill . . ."

Three times there was one for Janice. She put them carefully on her desk. After she was through being postman, she sat down and opened them.

One was a pink satin heart; it came from Miss Merrill.

The second was a picture of a basket full of hearts; she didn't know who had sent this.

The third one was big, and the envelope was made from drawing paper.

"I wish this could be from Margaret," Janice thought. "But it can't be. Her valentines were red, and anyway there wasn't one for me."

She opened it slowly, then stared in surprise. The class, she realized, was looking at her. Margaret especially was looking . . . and trying not to laugh. In a moment Janice knew why.

The valentine was the picture of a snowman, drawn with black crayon. He was

smoking a pipe. On his head he wore a red valentine cap. Snowflakes had been drawn with crayon also, and there were two girls in snowsuits ... one blue and one red ... dancing wildly in the snow. At the bottom of the page Margaret had written: "For my Snowstorm Valentine."

"It's from me," Margaret whispered. "I made it when you went out with Bobby. Do you like it?"

"It's wonderful," Janice said.

Smiling, she folded it and placed it in her purse next to the valentine Mary Lou had sent her.

After the Valentine Box they played games. And after the games they had refreshments. They had ice cream and cake and little candy hearts. Janice saved a heart to take home to her mother.

It was a lovely party, but not so nice as what came after.

She and Margaret walked home together. It had stopped snowing; the wind had died down, and sunshine sparkled on the drifts.

"Can't you come over to my house and

play?" Margaret asked. "We could make a big snowman just like the one we saw today."

"I'll ask Mom," Janice answered.

So they stopped at Janice's house, and Janice said, "Mom, this is Margaret, my Snowstorm Valentine."

At that, she and Margaret burst out laughing, and Janice's mother laughed, too. She asked Margaret, "Did you come out of the Valentine Box?"

That made Janice and Margaret laugh harder than ever, and they went to Margaret's house and played.

About the Author

MAUD HART LOVELACE has written many books—some of them with her husband, and some, like *Early Candlelight,* for adults—but her largest audience has always been the thousands of American children who have read and loved her Betsy-Tacy series and her other books for boys and girls.

Mrs. Lovelace was born in Mankato, Minnesota, and attended the University of Minnesota. She married Delos W. Lovelace, who was a lieutenant in a machine-gun battalion during World War I and afterward became a newspaperman and writer. The Lovelaces lived for some time in New York City, where their daughter Merian was born. When Merian was old enough to listen to stories, Mrs. Lovelace began telling her tales of her own childhood in Mankato, which grew into the Betsy-Tacy books.

Out of these books, which take Betsy from her first school day to her marriage, has sprung a wide correspondence between Mrs. Lovelace and children of all ages and backgrounds. This tie with young people is, she feels, one of the happiest rewards of her work.

Mr. and Mrs. Lovelace now live in California.

About the Illustrator

INGRID FETZ's illustrations have appeared in magazines, newspapers, and books. However, she considers her primary interests to be children and books. She has taught art to children and adults, and was Director of the Cambridge, Massachusetts, Art Center for Children for a number of years.

Miss Fetz attended the Cambridge School of Art, Columbia University, and the Workshop School of Advertising and Editorial Art. She lives in Ossining, New York.